SPECIAL FRIENDS WITH SPECIAL NEEDS

KATHY CHARLEY

*Kathy Charley*

*September 17, 2016*

Dedicated to my mother and best friend, Jeanne

# Acknowledgements

I will be eternally grateful to George Andrews at ROISem.com. He designed and implemented my website, video and viral marketing. Without him, none of these things would have been possible. The quality of his work is unsurpassed. He will be there to help me on all future endeavors.

I literally searched the world to find the artist who could catch the vision and essence of the characters in my book. I found her, Claudia Gadotti, in New Zealand at claudiagadottiart.com. She will always have my heartfelt thanks and will be the artist for all of my future books.

It took an exhaustive search to find the perfect editor, one who could edit my work and, yet, keep it mine. Emily Heinlen Davis did just that. Her editing is superb. She also formatted and converted my book for online publication. I wouldn't trust my work with anyone else and she will be the one to work on all of my future books and

publications. She can be found at emilyheinlen.com.

## Preface

The first part of my career was spent in the business world. I have done everything from being an account representative handling other companies' accounts to helping organize and manage a four million dollar company to owning my own companies. The last 11 years of my career, I was a cardiovascular specialist, but my true passion and desire has always been writing.

I am finally at a point in my life where I am able to concentrate on my writing. I started writing two books: a novel and a motivational book for adults to help them overcome loss and abuse. Then, I realized that I had to do something that I have wanted to do since the 80s, write a children's book for children with special needs.

I wanted to do something to make a difference in the lives of children with special needs. I knew that I could do that through my writing. I have never written for children before, but this experience has been one of the most fulfilling and joyful experiences of my life.

I plan to have my book published, but my main goal is to market it to hospitals, schools, churches, libraries and numerous other organizations in order to get it into the hands of the ones who need it the most: children.

# Introduction

This story is about Timothy, a little boy who gets hit by a truck and ends up in a wheelchair for the rest of his life. You can imagine the isolation, loneliness and depression that this little boy feels while looking out the window watching his friends running and playing, knowing that he will never be able to do these activities again. Martin, his best friend, sticks by him even when his other friends get bored and move on. As they go along day-by-day, they meet other children with special needs and form a special group of very special friends. Then, they teach each other just how special they really are and they realize that they aren't different. They are actually quite special and unique.

Their school peers who used to laugh, point and make fun of them or just stare become so inspired by them, their kindness and the fun they are having that they want to become part of their group. This brings the children, school, community and even surrounding communities together.

Each of the special friends has a very special dream. The little group of friends and the other children in school help to make each one of those dreams come true.

This book is the first book in a series. The other books will follow the friends as they encounter bullying, abuse, drugs and all of the other issues that children are faced with today. Won't you join me on a journey through their lives? Read and learn how these small children teach a very big lesson in love, life and humanity.

# Table of Contents

# Unexpected Beginning

Timothy loved his brand new bicycle. It was bright and shiny and, on it, he could go very fast. He decided to name it Flash. One day, while riding Flash, Timothy spotted his friend Martin riding his bike on the other side of the street. Timothy called out Martin's name, but Martin didn't hear him. So, Timothy peddled faster. He knew that he should stop and look both ways before crossing the street, but he was in such a hurry that he just dashed across the street instead. He didn't see the big truck coming up behind him and the driver of the big truck didn't see him.

Soon, an ambulance arrived, blaring its siren and flashing its lights. In a hurry, the paramedics loaded Timothy into the back and sped him to the hospital. After Timothy had been at the hospital for a while, the doctors sat his parents down and told them that he would be in a wheelchair for the rest of his life. Timothy thought a wheelchair sounded like a lot of fun. His friends could push him really fast or he could wheel his chair on his own and fly down the street, just like on a bicycle. However, he soon found out that being in a wheelchair wasn't going to be a lot of fun. His friends soon got bored with pushing him in his chair and stopped asking him to play with them. He would sit at the window for hours watching his friends running, playing and doing all of the things that he couldn't do anymore. He looked at his picture on the table and then wheeled himself to the mirror and looked at himself now. Timothy started to cry.

His parents bought him presents and toys, but they didn't fill the need that Timothy had to do the things that his friends could do. He couldn't walk to school anymore and couldn't ride the bus with his friends. His mother took him to school in a special van that would lift him in his chair so that he could roll inside. When they arrived at the school, all of the other children would stare at him as he was riding the lift out of the van. Then, they would run off laughing and squealing into the school. Timothy would roll himself into the school behind the other children, but they were always so much farther ahead of him because they could go faster. He had to sit in a special place in the back of the room by himself because his wheelchair took up so much space. Even in a room filled with other children, he felt all alone.

Then, one day, his parents brought home a little kitten named Mikey to be Timothy's playmate. Timothy would watch Mikey for hours. The playful kitten would pounce and jump on his pink mouse toy before lifting it in the air, throwing it on the floor and starting all over again with the game. Once, Mikey spotted a ball of yarn and waited for just the right moment before attacking. He would often stare into space, his big green eyes searching for something. His ears were always twitching, listening to every sound. Sometimes, he would lie down, tuck his legs up under him, like only cats can do, close his eyes and take one of his many daily catnaps.

While Mikey slept, Timothy would roll his chair over to the window to visit with his other little friend, Freddie, the squirrel. He opened the window and then looked out and called for Freddie. Timothy always kept peanuts on the table next to the window and Freddie knew that when Timothy called, he would get a peanut, so he came running. Jumping from one tree and branch to another, the little squirrel raced as fast as he could to the window.

One day, as Timothy watched and waited for Freddie, he heard Martin call his name from the street. Martin was Timothy's only friend who still came to visit him. He didn't come as often as Timothy would like, but Timothy understood that he couldn't do all of the things that Martin could do. When they played now, it had to be something that they could do sitting down. Timothy smiled and signaled for Martin to come on into the house.

The boys smiled and did their handshakes and bumps that boys do to greet each other.

"Did you see the moving van that went down the street yesterday?" Timothy asked Martin.

"Yeah, a new girl moved in three blocks down. She has something on her legs."

"What do you mean 'something on her legs'?" Timothy asked.

"Metal things. Some kind of braces or something," Martin said with a confused look on his face. "She walks kind of funny, too. I think she might have something wrong with her like….."

"Like I do?" Timothy asked with sadness in his voice. "Maybe we should go meet her? Do you want to go now?"

"Sure. Hey, I'm sorry. I didn't mean to hurt your feelings."

"I know. I understand. It's just the way it is. I just have to get used to it, I guess," Timothy said.

The two boys stared at each other and then they started laughing, and they laughed until they couldn't laugh anymore. Then, Martin stepped behind Timothy and started pushing his wheelchair for him, even though he didn't have to as it was electric and could move on its own. However, they were best friends and he'd do anything for his best friend.

## A New Friend

They stopped in front of the house that Martin had seen the new girl and her family move in to. Once they arrived, they were unsure of what to do, so they just stood there for a while. Then, they looked at each other and then back to the house. Just then, Martin and Timothy noticed a girl standing in the window staring at them. Timothy waved at her. At first, she just continued to stare and then she smiled and waved back. Timothy and Martin looked at each other and smiled before heading toward the door. They didn't knock. They just waited for her to open it. Soon, the door opened to reveal the girl from the window. Timothy and Martin smiled at her and then let their eyes drift to her legs. The girl looked at Timothy's wheelchair, raised her head and said, "Hi, my name is Beth."

"My name is Timothy."

"My name is Martin."

"You're different from us," Beth said to Martin.

"I'm different?" he asked.

"Yes, you're not like me and Timothy. I know we are supposed to be the ones who are different, but I prefer to think of us as special."

"Special, I like that," Timothy said. "That's what we will call ourselves from now on."

Timothy suddenly felt whole again and Martin finally understood. Each of the friends was different and each of the friends was special. This moment was the first moment of a lifelong friendship. On that first day, they laughed and talked for hours. Then, they agreed that they would meet to go to school together in the morning. Beth went back inside her house, Timothy rolled his chair toward his house and Martin started running home. All three had smiles on their faces.

Going to school together became a habit. Each day, they would meet in front of Beth's house. Beth would sit on the arm of Timothy's chair and Martin would push. They each had their part.  They were together on the weekends, too. As a matter of fact, they were together as much as possible. The kids at school didn't stare at them anymore. They blended in just like everyone else. Soon, it was summer break. They played in the park, went to the movies and did all of the things that the other children did. They could do these things because they helped each other. What one couldn't do, the others could help them do.

When school started up again, they went back to their old routine. Only, when they got to school, something was different. There was a new boy in school. His name was Eddie and Eddie was different, too. He wasn't in a wheelchair and he didn't have crutches, but he looked different. He didn't have any hair. His head was completely bald. Timothy, Martin and Beth saw some kids across the hall pointing and laughing at Eddie, so they moved toward him and surrounded him.

"Hi, my name is Timothy."

"My name is Martin."

"My name is Beth. What's yours?"

A big smile spread across the boy's face. "My name is Eddie. I guess you want to know why I'm bald."

"No," the three children said in unison. "It doesn't really matter to us. Does what is wrong with us matter to you?"

"No," Eddie said. At that moment, he decided that he didn't need to tell them that he was bald because he had cancer.

Now, there were four special friends.

One day, on the way home from school, Eddie asked the others, "Did the kids at school ever stare at you before the three of you became friends?"

"Of course, and it hurt our feelings. It made me not want to go outside or go to school. Sometimes, they would laugh and say mean things," Timothy said. "But, once Martin and I met Beth, we realized that we weren't different. We're special. Then, the things that they said and did didn't bother us anymore. I guess they could tell because they stopped doing those things and started treating us just like everyone else. They will probably treat you that way too now that you are friends with us."

Eddie thought about that for a minute and then said, "When I first found out that I had cancer, I felt like I was weird and strange and I didn't tell any of my friends. I was afraid of what they would think or say. Then, when my hair started falling out, I didn't want to go out or have anyone see me. I would wear a hat everywhere I went, but, in school, they won't let you wear hats. At my last school, the kids were really mean and laughed at me. I thought it would be the same here. I was really scared on that first day of school, but then you three helped me and I suddenly knew that I was going to be alright."

They all nodded their heads in agreement because they knew just how he felt. Then, they all smiled because they realized that they didn't have to feel that way

anymore.

## And Then There Were Five

The months passed and soon it was summer again. One day, Timothy and his group of special friends were sitting in the park when one of their classmates walked over to them.

"Hi, my name is George," he said.

"I know who you are," Timothy said. "You go to our school, but you've never talked to me before. Why do you want to now?"

"I watched you and your friends at school last year. You always had so much fun and were laughing all the time, even if you are……"

"Are what? Different? Well, we don't think we're different. We think we are special. We don't care what anybody at school thinks. We used to, but we don't anymore. We are best friends and that means more than the other kids at school making fun of us. Why do you want to talk to us anyway?"

"I have a brother who is 'special.' He has something called Down syndrome. He looks different than the other kids and he acts different, too, but he's amazing. He's cute and funny and he's so gentle and nice to everyone. However, the kids at school and in the neighborhood laugh at him. I've told them to leave him alone or I will make them leave him alone. I just thought that....well, I just thought that maybe he could be friends with you and your friends."

This time, Beth answered, "Of course, he can. That's why we are all together. What's his name?"

"His name is Ricky. He doesn't go to our school. He has to go to a special school, but the kids at our school see him when my mom comes to pick me up, or when they are walking home from school and pass our house. Sometimes, they point at him and laugh. It really hurts his feelings because he doesn't understand. It makes him cry."

"They won't do that to him if we are around," said Martin. "We will be sure to be seen with him so that all of the other kids know that he is with us."

George had a puzzled look on his face. Then, he asked Martin, "What do you have wrong with you? I mean, why are you a part of this group? I don't see anything different about you."

Martin replied, "I was friends with Timothy first before anyone else joined us. I don't have a disability or a special need, but I'm different because I'm different than them because I don't. Get it?"

"Yeah, I think I do. That's kinda cool actually. So, if I give you my address, will you stop by, meet Ricky and take him places with you?"

They nodded their heads as one. "We will come by tomorrow after school," Timothy said.

"I…um….well…… thanks," George mumbled, looking down at the ground. Then, he looked back up at

Timothy and his friends and smiled. It was the best George had ever felt. He loved his little brother and now he knew that he would be ok.

The next day, the special group of friends made their journey to add another member. They rang the doorbell and George answered the door.

"Hi, come on in. Ricky is really excited about meeting you."

The four friends stepped inside the house. They heard the sound of running footsteps and then saw Ricky. He was so happy and excited; it made them all feel proud to be there. He won their hearts immediately. George was right. Ricky had a wonderful, happy personality and a smile that lit up the room. Yes, they would protect the newest member of their group. Now, there were five special friends.

## A Dream Come True

Summer vacation went by quickly and, soon, everyone was back at school. To Timothy, it seemed like all of the boys his age were playing a sport. He had always wanted to run track. He could run very quickly, or he used to be able to. He would sit and watch the track team practice for hours. It was fun to watch and he enjoyed it, but it hurt too because he couldn't run anymore. One day, one of the boys ran over to where Timothy was sitting. It made Timothy uneasy and sort of scared. He didn't know what the boy was going to do and the boy was much bigger than Timothy.

"My name is Max," the boy said. "I've seen you sitting here every day at practice. Guess you wanted to run track, huh?"

Timothy nodded his head and looked down at the grass.

"Well, I've got an idea. How fast can that thing go? Want to show me?"

Timothy could tell by the boy's voice that he wasn't trying to be mean; he was just curious.

"Sure," Timothy said, "but it doesn't go very fast. Not fast enough to keep up with you, anyway."

"Doesn't matter. Just show me. What do you say?"

Timothy said he would, but he still didn't completely trust the boy. He rolled down to the track, but when he tried to roll, the dirt track slowed him down even more. He could feel tears filling up his eyes, but he couldn't let Max see the tears. He'd think he was a crybaby.

"Well, that isn't going to work," Max said. "Let's go back up to the parking lot and you can show me there."

Once they got to the parking lot, Timothy showed Max how fast his chair would go.

"Hey, that's pretty fast," Max said with a smile on his face. "Tell you what. My dad is a builder and he might be able to get us something that we could lay around the track that you could roll your wheelchair on. Wanna try?"

Timothy's heart started beating so hard and fast that he thought it was going to jump right out of his chest. He might be able to run track after all. Not the same way as the other boys, but that didn't matter to him. Racing around the track was all that mattered to him. He smiled, clapped his hands and whistled. Max put his hand up in the air and the boys fist bumped each other.

"Why are you doing this for me? You don't even know me. Besides, most guys either ignore me or make fun of me. I don't understand," Timothy said.

"I was raised to treat everyone equally and, besides, it could just as easily have been me in that chair," Max replied. "It could happen to anyone. Not only that, but I've watched you and your friends together at school. You're always helping each other and you always seem to be having so much fun together. You could all be sitting at home feeling sorry for yourselves, but you're not. You're living life to the fullest and being kind to one another. I respect you for that. I'd like to be your friend and a friend to your friends, if you don't mind, that is."

Timothy put his hand out to shake hands with Max. "You are now my official friend. The others will all want to be your friend, too. You're a nice guy, Max. Thank you for doing this for me."

The boys made plans to see each other at practice and, as soon as Max's dad could find something to help Timothy, they would set it up on the track.

The next day, Max went to see the track coach. He told him what he wanted to do. He explained that he knew that Timothy couldn't really compete at any track meets, but he wanted him to be able to race with the team in practice. The coach told him that they could do it, but whatever they were going to put down for Timothy to roll on needed to be something that could be removed and it couldn't damage the track. He told Max that he needed to see and approve it before they used it. Then, he told Max how proud he was of him because he was the perfect example of a true team player.

Three days later, Timothy went to the practice field and saw Max and the other players laying something down around the track. Timothy whistled and Max looked up. The two boys waved at each other and smiled. Max signaled for Timothy to come over to the track.

"This is something my dad uses on his construction sites. It's not perfect, but it will help your chair roll easier. We're almost through putting it down. Then, you can try it."

Timothy was smiling so wide that his face hurt. Soon, Max signaled to him that they were ready for him to try it. Timothy rolled onto the plastic. He put his chair at top speed and quickly began spinning on the plastic.

"No, no," Max yelled. "You have to ease into it. Then, you can go full speed. You'll need to remember that this plastic isn't like being on a sidewalk or driveway. It's a lot slipperier. You'll need to go slower until you get used to the feeling of rolling on it."

Timothy nodded his head in agreement. He slowly gave the chair some power. Then, he gave it a little more and a little more. Soon, he became used to how it felt rolling on the slippery surface and he started to go faster and faster. All of a sudden, his chair started to slide on one of the turns. He couldn't stop it. He'd never had this happen before. He'd never been on anything that he could slide on. He was really scared. The chair slid off of the plastic and hit the dirt, causing it to stop so quickly that Timothy went flying.

Max watched in fear as Timothy went flying through the air. He ran as fast as he could. All of the boys did. When they got to Timothy, he was lying on the ground with his arms and legs every which way. Max leaned over him and was just about to ask if he was all right, when Timothy burst out laughing.

"That's the most fun I've had in a long time."

He laughed harder and, then, Max started laughing with him. Soon, all of the boys began laughing so hard that they fell onto the ground next to Timothy.

Max said, "I'll have to ask my dad what we can put on the plastic to stop you from sliding, but we will figure it out."

Then, several members of the team high fived Timothy. It was at that moment that he knew that he was part of the team. His heart burst with joy.

Two days later, Max signaled to Timothy to come over to the track. His dad had a product that they could spray on the plastic to give it a no slide finish. This time, when Timothy started around the track, he got up to top speed without any problems. When he got back to the team, they were waiting to run the second lap with him. Off they went, Timothy in his chair and the rest of the team running.

## Leading the Band

The next day Timothy couldn't wait to tell his friends. He was so excited and talking so fast that they had to tell him to slow down because they couldn't understand him. They were all so happy for him. The boys high fived him and Beth hugged him. However, Timothy noticed that Beth had a sad look on her face. He asked her what was wrong. She told him that she was happy for him, but, at the same time, it reminded her of what she couldn't do. She had always wanted to be the baton twirler who led the school band. She even had her own baton that she practiced with at home, but it was just a dream that she knew couldn't come true. Her friends stared at her with sad faces.

Timothy broke the silence by saying, "If my dream can come true, then so can yours. Don't you dare give up hope! We have all had our dreams come true by just getting to be friends. It made all of our lives better. So, if that can happen, then anything can."

That statement brought a smile to her face. Timothy was right. She wouldn't give up hope.

The next day, Timothy met Max at the track.

"Max, I need your help. You made my dream come true and I have a special friend who really needs help to make her dream come true. I feel bad asking you for help after you just did so much for me, but I don't know who else to go to. I don't expect you to be able to make it happen, but maybe you could tell me who could help. If you know someone, maybe you could help me talk to them. They would probably listen to you, but I don't think they would want to help me."

"Look, little buddy, you are my friend and I'll do whatever I can to help you and your friends," Max said. "But I don't want you to think that no one would want to help you. Haven't you noticed how different the other kids at school treat you now? They have all seen what I've seen. I told you how much I respect you and your friends for how you treat each other and everyone else. You are all such good examples to the rest of us on how to live our lives. I've heard people talk at school and they admire you, too. Anyone who doesn't admire you is a bully and probably doesn't respect himself. So, we will talk about this issue and try to figure out how to help your friend. I will go with you to talk to whoever we think might help, but you need to be the one to ask them because you need to see and understand that they want to help you, too. Is it a deal?"

Timothy and Max shook hands and then sat down to think and talk. He explained to Max how Beth wanted to be a baton twirler, but didn't think she could because of her braces. They finally came up with a solution and set off to find the person who could help them make it a reality.

Almost two weeks later, Max told Timothy to have Beth on the football field when the band was ready to practice.

"Hurry," Timothy said to his friends. "Follow me and don't ask any questions."

He nodded at Martin, which was the signal for him to give Beth a piggyback ride so that they could go faster.

When they got to the football field, everyone, but Timothy and Martin, looked around trying to figure out why they were there. Timothy put his hand out to stop Eddie and Ricky from going further. Martin kept going with Beth. They walked past the band members to a little group forming a circle. All of a sudden, the circle opened up and Beth saw the platform that they were standing around. It was small and had a stand in the middle with a wide belt attached to it. It even had a little motor that could be used to move the platform. Tears ran down Beth's face. She had figured out what the stand was for. Martin set her down on the platform and put the belt around her, fastening it tight so that she wouldn't fall when it moved.

"You push the button with your foot. Do you think you can do that?" Max asked.

Beth nodded her head.

"You can twirl your baton while you're moving, as long as the ride is smooth. If it gets bumpy or if you are ready to toss the baton into the air, you can just stop until you are ready to move again. Got it?"

"Yes," Beth said, barely able to get the word out. "Thank you, Martin." She looked around at the rest of the group and then smiled and waved. Her dream had come true.

## Eddie's Wish

They watched as Beth led the band around the field. Timothy heard Eddie say very softly, "My dream would be not to have cancer."

Timothy thought about Eddie's dream for a while and then said, "I can't cure your cancer, but I have an idea of what might help for now. Who knows, maybe someday I can help cure your cancer."

"What do you think you can do?" Eddie asked.

"It's a surprise. If I can pull it off, then I think you might like it." Timothy was already making plans to help Eddie. He wasn't sure if he could do it or if it would work, but he was going to try.

That night, Timothy asked his mother, "What do you have to do to get a wig?"

"What?" his mother asked. "Honey, what in the world are you talking about?"

He told his mother all about Eddie and what he had said. Then, she understood. She told him that she would have to check and see what a wig would cost and where to get one, but she warned him that it would probably cost a lot of money. She looked at her son with so much love and pride. She decided that she would find a wig for him to give to Eddie.

The next afternoon when Timothy got home from school, his mother walked into his bedroom. He looked up at her, his eyes got big and his mouth dropped open.

"Mom, what did you do to your hair?"

Her usually shoulder-length, blond hair was now short and brown. While he was watching her, she reached up and pulled the wig off her head. They both started laughing. Then, Timothy rolled his chair to his mother, put his arms around her and hugged her tightly.

"Thank you, Mom! Was it expensive?" Timothy asked.

"You let me worry about that. You just surprise Eddie with it and, if it makes him happy, then that's all I care about."

"Mom, you're the best!"

His mother smiled and said, "Well, you remember that the next time I tell you to do your homework." As she walked out of his room, she turned, looked at her son and smiled.

Timothy couldn't wait to get to school the next day. He had the wig safely tucked in his backpack when he met up with his friends. At lunchtime, they were all gathered at their usual place to eat.

"What are we doing after school?" Timothy asked.

They looked at each other and shrugged their shoulders.

"Then, I've made a decision," Timothy said. "I say we all go to Eddie's house."

Eddie looked at Timothy and raised his eyebrows. "What are you up to?"

Timothy winked at Eddie and then he pushed his chair away from the table to put his lunch tray on the counter. The other three just watched him. They were each lost in their own thoughts about what he was planning. Eddie knew that it had something to do with him, but he didn't know what it could be.

When they got to Eddie's house, they were all excited to see what Timothy's secret was going to be. Ricky met them there and he was more excited than anyone. A secret was something magical to Ricky. He couldn't sit down and he couldn't stand still. He just smiled, clapped his hands and turned in circles. Timothy stood in the middle of the living room.

"Ready?" Timothy asked. Then, he reached into his backpack, pulled the wig out, walked over to Eddie and slid it on his head.

Eddie couldn't even speak. He just sat there with his hands on his new hair. Then, he jumped up and ran to the bathroom. He looked in the mirror and his eyes filled with tears. He looked like he used to and, for a minute, he didn't have cancer anymore.

"Let's see, Eddie," the others yelled. Ricky ran down the hall yelling, "Let's see." He stopped at the bathroom door and stared. "You look beautiful," he told Eddie. One-by-one, the others all peeked in through the door. Soon, tears were running down their faces, but they were tears of joy.

Then, there were only two wishes left unanswered.

## Changing Schools

When they were all back in the living room sitting and talking, Martin looked at Ricky and asked, "So, Ricky, what is your wish?"

"I get a wish?" Ricky asked.

"Of course, you do," Beth said.

"I wish I could go to school with you."

Beth looked at Eddie. Eddie looked at Timothy. Timothy looked at Martin.

Timothy was the first one to speak. "Have you told your parents that?"

"No," Ricky said. "They talk sometimes. I hear them. They think it's better where I am, but I don't. I don't want to be better. I want to be in school with you."

"Maybe," Martin said, "we can get the principal at the school to talk to them. I don't know if it would help, but would you like us to try?"

Ricky jumped up in the air like a rabbit. He jumped and clapped with a smile on his face so big that it went from one ear to the other.

"Yes, yes, yes, yes, yes, please, please, please!"

This request was not going to be as easy a dream to make come true as the others had been and they all knew it, but that wasn't going to keep them from trying.

The next day, while George kept Ricky busy at the park, the other four children went to speak to Ricky's parents.

Timothy told Ricky's parents about the wishes that had come true. Then, he told them about Ricky's dream. They were very quiet while he talked and even for a while after he had finished. Jan, Ricky's mother, spoke first.

"I know you are trying to help and you think you know what is best for Ricky, but we are his parents and we know what is best for our son. He needs to be in a school where he can get the extra time from his teacher that he needs. We want him with other children who are just like him so that no one stares at him or upsets him. We think that it is very nice of you, Timothy, to care about our little Ricky, but he is where he needs to be."

"But you don't understand. The kids at school don't stare at us anymore. They are our friends. They like us and Ricky belongs with us," Timothy said sadly. "Please, would you just talk to Ricky? Would you come to our school and see what it's like?"

"I don't know, Timothy. We can't just let Ricky make his own decisions and coming to your school for a few minutes isn't going to tell us anything," Frank, Ricky's father, said.

Timothy closed his eyes and shook his head. How could he get them to understand? He knew that there was nothing more he could do right then. He had to be respectful of Ricky's parents. He just didn't know how he was going to tell Ricky. He thanked them and then drove his chair home very slowly and very sadly. When he got home, he told his mother what had happened. She put her arms around him and told him that he couldn't always solve everyone else's problems. Sometimes things just didn't work out the way we wanted them to or thought they should. She told him that things had a way of always working out for the best and he just needed to give it time.

The next day on the way to school, Timothy told the other three what Ricky's parents had said. They were all sad. How could everyone get their wish except for Ricky? They walked the rest of the way to school in silence.

After school, they met up with Ricky. He didn't want to play or laugh. They had never seen him like that before.

Day after day went by and Ricky was the same. Finally, Martin said to Ricky, "If you are so sad because you can't come to our school, then you have to make your parents understand. Do you know how to do that?"

"No," Ricky said quietly. "They know I'm sad. They say that I will be happy again, but I don't think so. I don't want to go to school anymore. I don't want to live there anymore."

"Wow," said Beth, "don't talk like that, Ricky. Your parents love you. You might not agree with them, but they are only doing what they think is best for you. What if we all go talk to them? Maybe we can get Principal Anderson to go with us. Would that make you feel better?"

Ricky jumped up and down and clapped his hands. Everyone smiled. He was happy again. They just had to make sure that they could make this work out for him. One-by-one, they looked at each other and took deep breathes that they let out slowly. Granting this wish was not going to be easy.

The four friends took Ricky home and told him that they would see him in the morning. He was much happier now. He just knew that his friends would find a way for him to go to their school.

They left Ricky and headed home lost in thought. Eddie was the first to speak. "I don't want you to think that I'm not grateful, but," and Eddie took the wig off his head, "I don't think I want the wig. Timothy, you can't hide your wheelchair. Beth, you can't hide your braces, and Ricky can't hide his Down syndrome. Why should I hide my cancer?"

None of them had thought about it like that before, but Eddie was right. Why should he? He should be proud of who he was and his fight against his cancer. They agreed. Timothy told Eddie that he would take the wig back to his mother, but that someday he might still find a cure for his cancer. Eddie was happy enough with that.

The next day at school, the little group went to see their principal, Mr. Anderson. He invited them into his office. He smiled at them and asked them what he could do to help them. They told him all about Ricky. He told them that he didn't know if he could change Ricky's parents' minds, but he would be glad to visit and talk with them. They begged him to try really hard. They were afraid that Ricky would never be happy again if he couldn't go to school with them. He promised that he would try his hardest. He said that he would call Ricky's parents tomorrow and see if he could make an appointment to visit with them. He would explain to them that Ricky could do just as well at their school as at his current school.

The next day when the four friends were getting ready to leave school, Principal Anderson stopped them in the hall and asked them to come into his office. He didn't look very happy.

"I'm sorry to say that Ricky's parents were not agreeable to meeting with me. They said that they already told you that they were not going to let him come to this school. They were rather upset that you had come to me and asked for help after they had told you no. I know this is bad news for you, but I don't think anything else can be done. Once again, I am very sorry, but I think you have to drop this subject and move on. Ricky is where his parents want him to be and they are the ones who make the decisions for him. I admire all of you for caring enough about him to come to me. As a matter of fact, I admire you for a lot more than that. You are very special children. You have set such a good example for everyone in this school by the way you treat each other and all of the students. I have seen how the other students have changed the way that they treat you and each other. You have made each one of them a better person. I want to thank you for that and all of the other kind and caring things that you do."

"Thank you, Principal Anderson," they said in unison.

Then, Timothy said, "We know that you did your best to try to help Ricky. We couldn't ask for anything more than that. I guess some things are just easier to fix than others. We will have to try to find a way to make Ricky learn to accept his parents' decision and realize that it is for the best for now."

"You are very wise children. You will find a way, I'm sure of that," Principal Anderson said. He stood up and walked them to the door.

As the days went by, the friends tried to get Ricky to hang out with them, but he refused. He didn't want to play or laugh. His parents were having trouble getting him to eat. He cried himself to sleep at night. Then, one morning when his mother went to his room to wake him up for school, he wasn't in his bed. She started calling his name and running from room to room. She woke Frank. He told her to call the police, while he put on his clothes. Then, he ran out the front door. He looked both ways for Ricky. He thought he saw him way down the street, so he ran after him and called his name.

When he got close to Ricky, he asked him, "Ricky, where are you going?"

"I'm going to the real school, "he said. "You can't stop me. I don't want to go to that other school anymore. I don't want to go home with you."

"Oh, Ricky," his father said. "I am so sorry. We were trying to do what we thought was best for you, but I guess we didn't really understand. Come on. We are going to go home and talk to your mother."

"Only if you promise me that I can go to school with Timothy and the others."

His father looked at him with love in his eyes and said, "I promise, Ricky." Then, his father picked him up, hugged him tightly and carried him home. Ricky's wish had finally come true.

George called Timothy to tell him the good news. Timothy called the others and told them. Everyone slept well that night.

## Martin's Special Wish

The next day when they were all gathered together and celebrating the good news, Eddie said to Martin, "You're the only one who hasn't had a wish come true."

"What is your wish?" asked Beth.

"My wish came true before anyone else's wish," Martin said with a big grin on his face. "My wish was to have friends in my life who I knew I could count on and who liked me for who I am. I have those friends in each of you."

Timothy and the others looked at Martin. They each smiled. They knew how lucky they were and they knew that they had each other as friends forever.

## Special Events

One day, while they were playing in the park, Timothy said, "I was thinking that we have all had our dreams come truc, but there are so many others who haven't and maybe never will. I think we should find a way to help other kids. We can't make everybody's dreams come true, but, maybe, we can find a way to get a bunch of kids together and do something fun. What do you think?"

"I think that's a great idea," Beth said. "Do you have something in mind?"

"No, not really," Timothy said with a puzzled look on his face. "What do you think? Anybody got any ideas?"

They sat down in a circle and started trying to think up ideas. They thought and thought.

Finally, Eddie said, "Well, let's see. It has to be something that everyone can do, but kids have different special needs, so everyone can't do the same thing. It also needs to be something fun. Timothy, you and Beth did something active. Eddie and Ricky didn't do anything that anyone else could do. So, that wouldn't work, but, maybe, we could do something with what you and Beth did."

"I've got it," Eddie said jumping up and dancing around. "You know how they do those Special Olympics on TV? What if we did something like that? We could call it Special Events!"

"I want to, I want to, I want to," Ricky yelled. He didn't know what the Special Olympics were, but it sounded like fun to him. "How do we do it?" he asked.

Martin explained to Ricky that the Special Olympics were made up of many games that children like them played. Ricky liked the sound of that. He was really excited now. Games were always fun for him. Now, they just needed to figure out what types of games they were going to play.

"What about wheelchair races?" Timothy asked. "Look what I got to do with the track team. Only this time, everybody would be in wheelchairs."

They all agreed on that one.

"We could have baton twirling," Beth added.

They weren't sure about that one. There might not be any other girls who liked to do that and they didn't think there would be many guys who would want to do that, but they agreed that they would offer it and see what happened.

"Have you ever played table tennis?" Martin asked Beth. "I mean, you couldn't run after the ball, but you could stand in front of the table and hit the ones that came in range. If there were other kids in braces or who weren't in wheelchairs, but still couldn't move around very well, that would be something they could try."

"I've never played before," Beth stated, "but I wouldn't mind trying. It's always good to learn new things."

They knew that wheelchair races, baton twirling and table tennis weren't enough activities, so they added basketball, volleyball and soccer to the list. Kids like Eddie, Ricky and Martin could play those games. They decided that the best thing to do was to make a sheet for each game and take the sheets to all of the schools and churches in town to try to get boys and girls to sign up. Then, they could see which games got the most signatures. They decided that it would be a good idea to go to all of the local grocery stores to ask for food and drink donations as well. This process was going to take some time and it was going to take a lot of help from their parents. They couldn't go to all of those places alone. They thought that they could put up signs in the neighborhoods around town saying where anyone interested could sign up. It might take a lot of work, but they thought it was worth it. Plus, they could charge admission and donate the money to a children's hospital.

They each talked to their parents that night and told them what they had planned. Their parents told them that they thought it was a wonderful idea, but it would take a lot of work and might not turn out the way they wanted it to. They would have to be prepared just in case they didn't get enough girls and boys to join. They would also have to figure out where they could hold the games and how to get the equipment they would need. It wasn't going to be easy, but their parents were very proud of them.

It was easy to get the kids to sign up at their school because everyone knew them, but when they went to other schools, it was hard to get anyone to listen. They hadn't seen Timothy racing the track team or Beth leading the band across the football field. They were going to need backup for the other schools. They were going to need help from Max and George.

The next day, the five friends met with Max and George and told them what they were trying to do and why they needed their help.

"Yeah, no problem," Max assured them. "I told you that I would be here for you. What do you say, Georgie Boy?"

"Yeah, I'll help and don't call me Georgie Boy."

They made plans to meet and go to the other schools together. Plus, Max was going to get some of the other guys at the school to help.

They spent the next several weeks getting people signed up for the Special Events. People in other towns and cities nearby heard about the Special Events and signed up as well. Finally, they had enough children signed up to plan the events. Now, they just had to get the equipment.

Their school offered the basketball court and said that the friends could use any equipment that the school had as long as they took good care of the equipment and returned it all when they were done with it. Principal Anderson also offered the school's running track and soccer field, but other schools offered their tracks and fields as well and they were nicer. Everything was turning out better than they had hoped. They had all of the equipment that they needed and had their pick of the fields, courts and tracks within the city to use. They decided that they would have to pick a school with a paved track for the wheelchairs to roll on and for the baton twirlers to ride on. Murphy High School had that kind of track and also had a really nice soccer field; it was even lit.

They met with Principal Clark of Murphy High School to talk to him about using their school to host the Special Events. He told them that the school would be more than happy to help them and the community. He even said that they could set up a volleyball court for them; it would just have to be in the grass. The friends agreed that such a court would be wonderful. The principal said that they were welcome to use the school's basketball court as well. One of the other schools donated a table tennis table and Principal Clark said that they had a stage in their auditorium that would be perfect for that.

Now they would only need the equipment from their school and possibly one or two more items and they would have all that they needed. They were very excited; this event was going to be the best event ever.

In the following weeks, they managed to find a printer to donate the tickets and flyers, and three grocery stores to donate snacks and drinks for them to sell.

Besides the original reason they had decided to do this event, the five friends learned another very important lesson. They learned how thoughtful, kind and helpful people could be when you just reached out to them. To think, they were worried that no one would want to help them. What they found out was that almost everyone did want to help.

The closer it got to the Special Events, the more excited everyone got. You could see boys and girls practicing in fields and front yards. The friends wanted to include everyone, so there were teams for children with special needs and teams for children without special needs. That way, everyone could have fun.

The day of the Special Events turned out to be a sunny, warm day. Timothy looked around at the crowds of people. He had never imagined that there would be so many people. They were everywhere. Everyone was laughing and having so much fun. The events were getting ready to begin. He turned and looked at his four best friends and smiled. He could hardly believe that the five of them had actually put this whole thing together. He thought about how that made him feel and realized that it made him feel whole again. It made him feel as if there wasn't anything he couldn't do. He liked that feeling. He decided right there and then that he was going to do another Special

Events, only next time, it would be even bigger and, maybe, include the entire state.

They were all happy and pleased with how the day turned out. Timothy didn't win the wheelchair race, but he was fine with that. Winning wasn't what mattered to him. He just wanted everyone to have fun. Beth did win the baton twirling. She was able to throw her baton higher than anyone else. She got to ride her stand around the track, waving at the crowds, with her medal around her neck. She was happier than she had ever been. Her four special friends were very, very proud of her. Eddie did really well at table tennis and decided that he might learn how to play tennis on an actual court. He did so well, in fact, that he won a medal. Ricky played soccer and had more fun than anyone. He didn't really know how to play, but that was the event he picked. He was so cute running around the field chasing the ball. People were surprised at how fast he was and how he beat the other kids to the ball most of the time.

Sometimes, he would kick the ball in the wrong direction, but it didn't matter. The point was that he kicked it at all. He didn't care that he didn't win or get a medal. All he cared about was getting to play. Martin played volleyball. He didn't win a medal, but he got a lot of the girls' attention. He was happy enough with that.

When all of the events were finished, Principal Clark got on the loud speaker. He called Timothy and his four friends to the speaker's platform. He told the crowd that these five children were the ones who were to be thanked for this wonderful, exciting and rewarding day. He said that between the ticket, food and drink sales, they had raised over $60,000 for the local children's hospital. When he said that, the crowd clapped and cheered so loud that it was deafening. The five friends just looked at each other in surprise. They had no idea that they had done so well. They started clapping and cheering as well. Then, they high fived and hugged each other. They had done it. They had shown

were spent trying to catch up on all of the errands for which she couldn't find time during the week.

She is now retired from the medical field and working as a part-time nanny. This position has provided her with the time necessary to devote to her writing. Instead of focusing on the two books she had already started, Kathy decided to do something that she had wanted to do since the 1980s; she wanted to help disabled children and she knew that she could do that through her writing. Thus, *Special Friends with Special Needs* came to fruition.

Kathy wanted to write a book for children that would be fun to read, but could also be used as a teaching and developmental tool. She wanted to write a book to give children self-confidence and self-worth and teach them kindness and compassion for others. Those values are what this special book is all about. She wrote it to reach children and instill in them the values and virtues that they will need to stand strong against all of the issues that they will have to face in the world as they grow older.

Kathy plans to self-publish *Special Friends with Special Needs*, but her main goal is to get the book into children's hospitals, schools, libraries and bookstores so that it can get into the hands of every child.

Made in the USA
Charleston, SC
21 August 2015